FEMININE VENOM

Our Story So Far...

Sanjak has successfully used Pat, Terry, and the gang to stop Baron de Plexus' plane filled with Chinese gold. Taking April Kane, which she has hypnotized, along with her, she lands in the jungle with Pat & Terry in hot pursuit. Even though she foils a clever attempt by Pat to nab her as she descends the jungle river, she has unwittingly left them as well as de Plexus clues to where she's going ...

ISBN 0-918348-40-4
LC# 87-090446

© NBM 1988
cover designed and painted by Ray Fehrenbach

Terry & The Pirates is a registered trademark of Tribune Media Services, Inc.

THE FLYING BUTTRESS CLASSICS LIBRARY
is an imprint of:

NANTIER · BEALL · MINOUSTCHINE
Publishing co.
new york

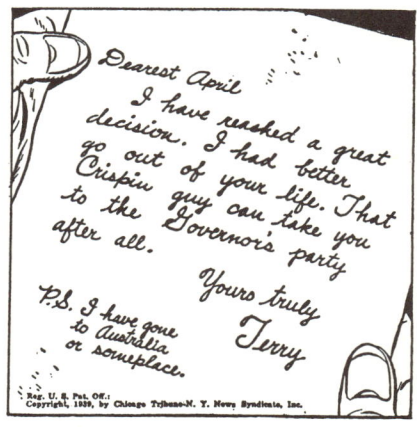

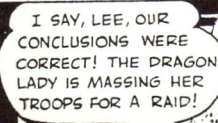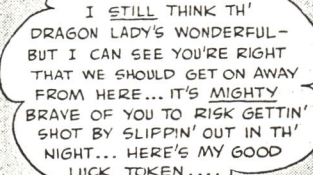

OTHER CANIFF BOOKS FROM NBM

TERRY & THE PIRATES "COLLECTORS' EDITION"
12 288-320 page, hardbound, gold stamped books reprint the complete *TERRY*. Every daily and Sunday strip, many never before reprinted, is shown in full size. Write for more information.

MILTON CANIFF - REMBRANDT OF THE COMIC STRIP
The original version of this book appeared in 1946 as Caniff was finishing his work on *TERRY*. Comic historian Rick Marschall has updated this 1980 edition. There are many rare and beautiful illustrations and blowups of Caniff art.   Paperback - $6.95.

MISSING ANY VOLUMES?
TERRY & THE PIRATES paperback reprinting chronologically from the beginning. Issued quarterly. Each 64 pp., 8 1/2x11, color cover.
Vol.1 Welcome to China (1934) $5.95
Vol.2 Marooned with Burma (1935) $5.95
Vol.3 Dragon Lady's Revenge (1936) $5.95
Vol.4 Getting Snared (1936-1937) $5.95
Vol.5 Shanghaied (1937) $5.95
Vol.6 The Warlord Klang (1937-1938)$6.95
Vol.7 The Hunter (1938) $6.95
Vol.8 The Baron (1938-1939) $6.95

NOW AVAILABLE: SUBSCRIPTIONS!
You can subscribe to 4 starting with any volume: $25 (free P&H).

ALSO: HANDSOME SLIPCASED SETS
4 Volumes in each for a total of 256 pages of intense reading slipcased in beautiful leatherette, gold stamped.
Vols. 1-4: $27.50
Vols. 5-8: $29.50
slipcase alone: $5

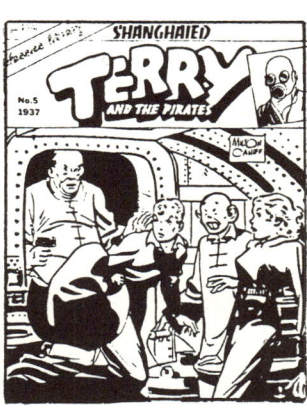

P&H: add $2 first item, $1 each addt'l.
Allow 6-8 weeks for delivery.

NBM
35-53 70th St.
Jackson Heights, NY 11372

Flying Buttress Classics Library
announces:

the complete

WASH TUBBS & CAPTAIN EASY

1924 – 1943

The Flying Buttress Classics Library, announces a new reprint: Roy Crane's classic *WASH TUBBS* (1924-1943). Wash Tubbs was Crane's first strip, and already with it he set the pace for future adventure strips to match, including Terry & The Pirates. Wash Tubbs exemplifies two-fisted adventure spiced with a good sense of humor. Wash and his pals, Gozzy Gallup and **Captain Easy**, battle arch villians Bull Dawson and Shanghai Slug in exotic locales on land and sea around the world.

Each volume of this quarterly **18 volume complete reprint** will contain 192 pages of action. Like our recently completed Terry & The Pirates series, you can count on high quality and regular publishing schedules. Both hardcover and paperback will be available in a large but handy 11 by 8 1/2 format. Each volume will print approximately one year's worth of strips. Sundays are included.

PAPERBACK EDITION
$16.95 each
(add $2.00 postage & handling)

HARDCOVER EDITION
$32.50 each
(add $2.00 postage & handling)

Vols. 1-4 available

SPECIAL OFFER:
Order your subscription to any 4 hardcover volumes and pay only $80!
Also available: you can subscribe to the paperback edition for $50 for **any** four. (no p + h for subs)

NBM
35-53 70th St.
Jackson Heights, NY 11372